**What is the difference between a prose poem and flash fiction?**

Flash fiction is a compact distilled piece of writing that follows all of the dictates (or lack thereof) that one would place on a work of fiction. It is an act of distillation. Of sparseness. Minimal strokes. A prose poem is often the very opposite. Where flash fiction is a working down of a form, prose poetry is an exploding up of a form, a release from structure, a star erupting, a channel run straight from the brain stem to the pen.

**Jonathan Carr**
***Double Room: A Journal of poetry and flash fiction***

This collection features writing by the following invited contributors: Dael Allison, Judith Beveridge, Peter Boyle, joanne burns, Michelle Cahill, Shady Cosgrove, Moya Costello, Anna Couani. Keri Glastonbury, Philip Hammial, Carol Jenkins, A. S. Patric, Vivienne Plumb, and Michael Sharkey.

The winning entries from the *small wonder* anthology competition chosen by joanne burns are published in this anthology.

Winner:                    Charles D'Anastasi

Commended:           Erin Gough

                               Clare McHugh

Also included are shortlisted entries by John Carey, Michael Farrell, Adam Ford, Monica Goldberg, Gregory A Gould, Stu Hatton, Jo Langdon, Kent MacCarter, Alyson Miller, Cara Munro, Aden Rolfe, Laurie Steed and Sean Wilson.

# small wonder

an anthology of prose poetry and
microfiction

edited by
Linda Godfrey and
Julie Chevalier

SPINELESS WONDERS

www.shortaustralianstories.com.au

Spineless Wonders
BN01164417
PO Box 220
STRAWBERRY HILLS
New South Wales, Australia, 2012
www.shortaustralianstories.com.au

First published by Spineless Wonders 2012

Cover image and illustrations (pp. 12, 24, 43, 50, 58, 71, 80, 83, 99, 101, 105 and 110) copyright © Paden Hunter 2012.

Copyediting and layout by Bronwyn Mehan.

Typeset in Bodoni MT

Printed and bound by Lightning Source Australia

ISBN 978 0 98708 978 6

# Contents

**Acknowledgements**

**Biographies**

# INTRODUCTION

The invitation to submit work to the *small wonder* competition set the parameters for what was included in this anthology. Here's what it said:

*Is it a prose poem? Or poetic prose? Perhaps it's postcard fiction or sudden prose. A vignette or a monologue. Spineless Wonders invites you to break some rules. Do some genre-bending. Let the line break take a stroll through the streets and fields of prose and surprise us with edgy, unexpected moments. Our judge, joanne burns, is looking for the small and stealthy. 800 words max.*

Expect synergy. When jazz fuses with another music style new energy is released. When the cuisines of different cultures merge, the combinations of flavours surprise and delight us. Of course the fusion of poetry and short prose creates a feast for our literary taste buds. Another burst of energy comes from the integration of the work of so many emerging writers with the work of widely published and respected authors.

Prose poems and microfiction can appeal to people with limited time who need a blast of colour and excitement. We can read one or two pieces and blow our minds in a short space before wandering off to the rest of our grey day.

We are conscious of the gender equity issues in Australian literary publication, but it can be tricky to achieve equal representation when a competition is blind judged, as this one was. *small wonder* consists of thirty-one poems by sixteen female writers and twenty-three poems by fourteen male writers. Phew.

And our warmest congratulations to Charles D'Anastasi, winner; Erin Gough and Clare McHugh, commended; as well as all those short-listed.

Spineless Wonders is a new small indie publisher dedicated to publishing innovative short fiction. This is our fifth book. We profusely thank all who have given permission for their writing to be published. We acknowledge that we have not been able to invite many of our favourite poets and prose writers to contribute to this anthology. Fingers crossed Spineless Wonders will provide further opportunities.

Our special thanks to joanne burns for her professional judging and her generosity in providing ideas. Thanks to Paden Hunter for his artwork.

Bronwyn Mehan is the driving force of Spineless Wonders, and this anthology. We thank her for her ideas, her energy, her expertise, all the thankless, petty, hard work needed to get this baby off the ground and into the hands of the reading, and listening, public.

**Linda Godfrey & Julie Chevalier**

**March 2012**

# JUDGE'S REPORT

The *small wonder* shortlist of seventeen works offers a range of prose poems/microfiction that impress with their various individual qualities, whether the text is closer to poetry—more focussed on language, image, contemplation, etcetera—or whether it performs more as narrative.

### Winner—'Madame Bovary' by Charles D'Anastasi

In just three paragraphs (or 'stanzagraphs') Charles D'Anastasi with writerly, succinct and graceful ease, creates a compelling, animated and extended vision of the lovers, based on the carriage scenes from Flaubert's novel *Madame Bovary*. Like a literary revenant, this vision appears to the narrator within the context of a poetry reading. In effect the author, D'Anastasi, has stream-lined the novel into a rhythmic prose poem. It is a private vision, known only to the text's narrator, not to those at the poetry reading. This judge–reader was drawn into the relentless, fatal otherworld of Madame Bovary and her lover, as if spellbound, like the narrator. D'Anastasi has almost conjured up as if via a quasi-literary séance the actual relentless sounds of the horses' hoofs (or 'hooves'). This winning entry also considers the 'world' of a poetry reading, without jarring the palpable Bovarian vision.

**Commended—'William Shatner vows to save the Great Basin Pocket Mouse' by Erin Gough**

This amusing microfiction by Erin Gough is a playful, quirky and trim narrative centred on a game between two women lovers, which involves their bodies and their different nationalities' inventions. One is Australian, and one is Canadian. As they announce various inventions, e.g 'Ute', 'Trivial Pursuit', they become more physically intimate with each other. Instant mashed potato is used to fine effect in this story. The narrative ends with a swift double victory for one of them. 'William Shatner vows to save the Great Basin Pocket Mouse' is an exemplary flash fiction.

**Commended—'Briefly' by Clare McHugh**

'Briefly' is a confident consideration, sometimes cautionary, of the range of meanings, associations, manifestations and scenarios involving the word 'short'. Clare McHugh cleverly flirts with the *small wonder* competition brief to write a short text, under 800 words. 'Briefly' is a versatile lexicon. It is amusing, witty, wry and revealing. McHugh aerates her text with a series of short statements, sentences and paragraphs.

**joanne burns**

**January 2012**

# DAEL ALLISON

## *dreaming poets dreaming*

what if a raft were to loom from the dark with an old man at the bow, his hand firm on the helm? what if they stepped on, the two poets from another world?

life could be like this, real but another dimension, darwin rising from a blackout like a blazing fish in beagle bay, the air a flux of water, ondaatje and neruda adrift on a tropic river, the silent helmsman steering past up-lit cyclone ruins, emerald palms and the edifice to government the locals call the wedding cake, nudging through the flotsam of unconscious men, the raft a smudge on a rippled mirror.

what if neruda asks why make this building voiceless when stars are shouting, and the raft, caught in an answerless current, turns and surges into the brazen gorge of mitchell street where the waters churn with roach butts and mcdonalds styrofoam, pods of slick-sheathed girls, men tattooed like coral trout, where backpackers spew beer from balconies and bouncers circle like sharks.

the ferryman steers past throb, ducks nuts, shenanigans, neruda enigmatic at the prow, ondaatje, silver eyes alight, lurching from side to side yelling *giddaymatehowyagoin*. a black taxi cruises past, frangipani swilling in its wake, someone shouts *getofftheroadyafuckwits*, apparitions loom blank-eyed and screaming, blood streams from glassing's jagged cuts. the poets cling grimly as they drift past the cocktail luxe of hanumans, the smokers clotted on the entertainment centre steps.

the flood ebbs, the raft eddies in a backwash of public housing, bottle shops, cheap car rentals, sudden quiet. clapsticks sound, ancient twig men sing the dark. waters whisper into sand, sand whispers into silence, a curlew cries the doors to dreaming open. the poets walk into the desert, deafened by the stars.

# nightburst

*Lights, Darwin Harbour 1957*, Ian Fairweather

men teeter on your edges darwin. strung to night's ebb-tide filament-tight, cockle eyes attune to nuance of fish, their dangling legs sway to the lurch and wash of wave. you have no authority darwin. your pier lights do not arrest the dark, your static starbursts are as blind as mangrove mud. only prescient larrakia see *lit bateau*'s shadow slip across the sandbar away from fanny bay and scuttle quick as cuttlefish into the channel's inky narrative of crocodiles and moonfish, barramundi, bombed ships, downed planes, disintegrating men. your strangling chrome-green, chrome-yellow outpost hell of people scumbles black behind me. wind squalls like a fretful child. water streams fluid as slapped paint out and out the ever-stretching gulf past east point past mandorah beneath charles point's baleful lighthouse stare. flung like a skipping stone into the timor current, flotsam shadow random arrow sucked into distance, released from land's tether into rising weather, freed from strangling green and suffocating kind, *leaving australia behind to face the empty seas.* and they will be as deep and true as reckitts blue.

# JUDITH BEVERIDGE

## *The book of birds*

It's Tuesday and I'm standing in the queue waiting to have my nature explained to me from the book of life which is called *The Book of Birds*. 'Where the heart rubs closest to the street there is a nest of grey pigeons.' 'Where the heart touches the infinite there is one feather of a dove.'

X has just finished and whispers in my ear 'I live closest to the wound and am a bleeding-heart pigeon. I am trying to grow the feathers of a nightingale under which still beats the heart of a bleeding-heart pigeon.'

I am now only five away from the front. One by one people come away whispering their secrets—'my heart just falls into the dust—where the heart just falls into the dust there is a squabble of geese.' Or, 'my heart lives in the face of rocks and on the backs of field mice—where the heart lives in the face of rocks and on the backs of field mice there is the single, penetrating eye of a hawk.'

Now, it is my turn. I sit down. I say that my heart is forever sitting on an egg that won't hatch. They hunt through *The Book of Birds*. I suddenly feel as if my soul were being built up bit by bit from the droppings of a vulture. Any minute I expect them to say 'vulture'—or, fearing the worst and nervous lest my friends should hear me called a 'spangled grebe' or 'scaly breasted weebill'. But a few minutes pass and they are still hunting through *The Book of Birds*. They try the index, the cross-references, the footnotes. They scan every page. Finally, they admit that they can find no meaning for me in *The Book of Birds*. Stunned, I grab the book and as a last resort check under 'pied drongo'. With some relief, nothing.

But I am distraught. I wonder at the meaning of this. I have to tell my friends something so I say—where the heart has no meaning there is none other than the true and perfect ornithologist (page 203, I say, to make it sound like a quote). They are adequately impressed.

On my way home, I check the bookstores to see if it was the most up-to-date edition. I contact the publishers for possible errors. Finally in desperation, I send a letter off to the author, the enlightened one out of whose wisdom the book was compiled. In my best handwriting and using a quill taken from the wing of an extinct cassowary.

A few days later, a package arrives. To my bewilderment I find no page references, no explanations. Instead, enclosed is a small incubator with a note wishing me luck, obviously scratched from the claw of a Prince Albert lyrebird from our wet, sclerophyll coastal region.

# *Address from the curved city*

For five years I've lived in the curved city. As I say this now, it is difficult for me to adjust to the particular geometry of your vowels, having spoken for so long nothing but the beautiful variations of the vowel 'O'. Flattening my tongue against the roof of my mouth, pushing my lips into an almost straight line is a dreadful discomfort. Think of the beautiful vowel 'O'. The only vowel whose symbol exactly articulates itself in the human body.

In the curved city, we are at peace knowing language and landscape pose no threat to each other's design. Our terraces, our cloisters, our alcoves, our libraries are no less impure in vocal than in visual form. You who live in a world whose language and architecture have a purely arbitrary relationship can have no understanding of our aesthetic. Only a language such as yours, demotic and crude, could allow the dishonesty of the statement: 'the vowel "O" is produced in the voice-box.'

It is the principle of the curved city that unless a person is attuned to a place by their very breath they cannot have true peace. We have discovered our peace through the beautiful vowel 'O'. We have discovered in the curved city a propinquity with our world that you can only minutely approach through cries of pain.

So perfect is the conception of the curved city that on my arrival my legs went from point to point, not in their usual linear way, but imperceptively via the circuitous. As if my whole body became immediately tuned in to the aesthetic. Since arriving, I have not once felt at variance nor thought of the place from which I came. Only now in speaking these words do I remember the streets, the vertical and horizontal escarpments, the houses, the corpses outstretched, the faces and the mouths contorting, the orders and the bodies massed into those unspeakable mounds.

# PETER BOYLE

## *In response to a critic's call for tighter editing*

A poet should be able to write outside of the human in all sorts of directions. The moon is one of them. Water that has just bubbled out of the earth is another. Of course they are distant cousins as intimately related as the wind and a sandgrain.

If I was the moon I couldn't practise what I would say. I would have to be empty and desolate. Everything would happen by instinct like tides responding to my slow ballet. I would be ignorant as a worn shoe condemned to dance forever over subterranean waters. My cratered eyes would guide me through space and my children would say, *Look, he comes from forever, he's on his way to forever. He's the one blind man whose walking stick is the glide of small fish over sand, the waterfall that flows simultaneously in both directions.*

# *Night poems 14/10–16/10, 2011*

A clattering sound echoes around me like prayer wheels set spinning by the sudden brushing of wings or the fingers of ghosts. The spirit says to me, 'You have three days in which you are completely free to move wherever you like. Only your body must stay here—it is under our custody, our surveillance, so it will be strapped and wired into this bed.' 'But how can I move if my body has to stay here?' 'You will work out ways,' the spirit says.

A first try and I find I'm moving along the corridor past the wards, about to enter an overpass I never knew existed above Macquarie Street and Martin Place. For a moment, remembering something essential, I return.

'But my daughter comes here to the bedside every day. How will I talk to her? I can't move my lips anymore. My eyes just stare out blankly across the room and my hands shake too much to write or signal. How will I let her know I am no longer in the bed but have moved on and am waiting for her in the park beyond?' 'It will take time,' the spirit says. 'If you persist carefully she will come to understand.'

And so I begin, knowing this is no small task but a matter of getting ready to communicate my only truly important poems, the ones that last beyond me. I will have to unlearn every cleverness, every borrowed technique, turn of phrase, allusion I've ever picked up. At this point it won't help to know Greek or Latin or Spanish, Chinese or German. Experiences of the world, imaginary locations, fictive personas all useless. I am here in Sydney alone, a rickety hospital with moss-covered sandstone slabs and green-painted drains at the Hyde Park end of Macquarie Street. Maybe I can stretch my consciousness as far as Circular Quay or the steps leading up to the Harbour Bridge. I have three days only to articulate these poems—unlike other poems, they are uniquely for my familiar guardian the enveloping air that, knowing me for so long, will recognise and accept them and for a handful of close loved ones whether living or dead.

This time moving forward onto the bridge over Macquarie Street I see the poet from Sydney University I always admired and envied, gone fifteen years ahead of me. I confess to him how much I have learnt from him, how little my own poems seem worth compared to his. He stops me, saying, 'I learnt a lot from you. It's obvious in my last book which I'll give you now—I could show you the passages that could only be written after reading you—but let me sign a copy for you first.' And at that he stepped aside, a few steps off the raised sandstone walkway that suddenly I remember should be called an aula, and hovering there he balanced in mid air, the only place he could comfortably write now, he told me.

# Reading Max Jacob in Taichung

for Philip Hammial

'*La terre entière brûlera*' (Folklore 1943)

What is it that one writes to the very end and how does one write it?

All day a sulphurous smoke moves across the construction sites. One imagines air and water laced forever with the thin-spun fire of vast turbines that grind the mountains into dust.

He wanders through a Paris of tour guides and monuments, of bishops and dignitaries, everywhere the old graceful formalities, the allure of progress, peace and serenity, the bureaucratic flow of language asserting the golden age, and always at street corners the bronze sound-chambers of wells, dark fountains of water from which rise regular and echoing the screams of hell. Attempting invisibility he glides between two-legged wolves who wear the masks of company managers, consultants on urban renewal, police chiefs and advisers on the purification of air. Small stars made from coughed venom spin like shiny barbs down the gutters that run at all times under our feet. Shrinking to the size of a newborn child, he glides between the monsters and the monsters, carrying inside him a round loaf of bread that has blazed and will blaze before and after our species.

Max Jacob in the last days before Drancy, I imagine one universal yellow star.

# The tree's ambition

A tree with the deep ambition of becoming an ant: long evenings in night school, first attempts at rapid movement, countless resits of *Thinking like a team* (Business Studies 5071).

One day the tree realises: becoming an ant requires the perfection of smallness. The tree would start by concentrating its being in a single leaf, a dry leaf, preferably, scored with old wounds. Next it would work on narrowing its life span, ideally to no more than a few intense hours.

The tree thinks: living like an ant means living inside death—so much industry, endless conferences on collaboration, decisions taken in micro-seconds. Death as a name for a species, a destiny.

Here, inside its bark, watching a tribe of ants, unable to join their purposive non-stop rush hour. The sadness of being a tree. Its branches fall back around it like a song of defeat.'Farewell boys, comrades of my dreams, I must sleep with my silence. Always trying to mouth the one green syllable, condemned to the dunce's chair. Me and my eternal shadow. My inability to organise a planet.'

# JOANNE BURNS

## *buffet*

he said he'd left the cheese roll on the sideboard. made it with his own hands he did. spread the butter. laid out the cheese and pressed the two halves of roll together. like a carpenter not a ploughman. it was his. he did not expect anyone to take it.

something ordinary turns into a dispute. the bland exacting habits of a suited thug in pinterville. his philosopher brother in an almost trenchcoat said he'd eaten it. deliberately. he wanted it. yes. he saw his brother put it on the sideboard earlier in the day. a tenacity hovers in the room.

the empirical cheese roll turns abstract. no blood flows in this fraternal, fastidious episode. all is cold indignation and accomplishment. there is no greek tragedy in which a cheese roll figures. you may thank zeus for that.

# *easy*

when you fall you sprawl on the pavement like a virgin swimmer. you lie there stretching for your glasses that have skidded out of reach.

you are yourself. you clamber up. vertical and mobile. your best move. the blood runs down your leg. you cross the road. you rise to the occasion.

a child falls into a wall. a school game. a rush of legs and hands pushing to be first. to touch the bricks. an urgency for home. eyebrow flesh splits open. a little needlework ahead. glasses snap and crackle.

how many falls to go. it is an awkward thing to count. to calculate.

a boy falls from the top of a city tower. a tall boy carrying a note in his pocket insisting god had given him permission to jump. you recollect him walking towards you from the back of the room to ask the meaning of 'vernacular'. you had been impressed.

falling is a kind of vernacular.

dust falls, dates fall, love falls.

when you fall you sometimes dream it is forever. easy as the weather.

# *literate*

here. hair floats down towards the floor in a morning's sunlight. time for a moment, like a surprise cadence stroking the throat.

white hairs that have stored a life. lives. frail akashic records. their descent to the hardness of floor boards will filch their timbres. flows and whisps of thought stranded. obliterated. do not underestimate diana and the growling hunger of her vacuum cleaner hounds.

the more you brush the more they fall. is there a stubborn beauty to be observed. in this eloquent decline.

# *wink*

there's always something falling into one of my eyes. usually the left one. dandruff flakes dropping in for a visit from an eyebrow's foliage. from in between the layers of the canopy. dropping down for some hydration. irritants arriving uninvited. hairs, invisible mites that catch the eye off guard. nothing with the prestige of an icarus. no deep aegean blue or brueghel's green in my ocular curves.

&&&

this eye turns red as if a fierce little theatre has taken posses-sion. red as an avenging god or demon. the chemist girl gasps against the diorama of the make up display. well, i'm not going to casualty. it's an allergic reaction to particles of paint scraped from the window ledge. a small flask of drops will be my exorcist.

&&&

last year i had my first flash and floater moment in my right eye. google was chockabloc with explanatory websites. flash and floater—not quite the same as surf and turf. the flash came first as i was having a post-shower epiphany about the prominence of death. i wondered whether all those heritage listed visionaries and mystics simply were victims of retinal mistranslation—something a visit to an eye hospital or an optometrist might have fixed. how dull the fact of the retina being affected by the hardening of the eye's vitreous jelly, compared with the aura of divine revelation.

this tiny floater i've grown used to. my own little arachne. not a regular visitor, but a modest soothsayer and spy. i can't feed it peas but it seems to thrive on migratory dandruff and morsels from the air.

### &&&

red veins of an eyeball. perhaps ship routes on a globe or life tracks that need clarification. do not be deterred by their colour. is danger so simple. forget the chiromancer of the palm. become a vasculamancer.

i see you now with your bloodshot eyes standing in the doorway holding a raw egg in a clear glass. the yolk so like a bright fruit suspended in the clear albumen. this was your hangover cure. i believed you. then. the hangovers stopped. the veins in your eyes displayed potential.

### &&&

p.s. in nineteen sixty eight i saw a production of 'king lear' at the wagga drama theatre. during the scene where gloucester's eyes were gouged out warwick and i, sitting in the second row, rolled jaffas on the floor.

# MICHELLE CAHILL

## *An exercise in magic realism*

Being a parent is like an exercise in magic realism. The little person who starts out as a clump of fertilised cells inside you, glued together by glycoproteins, whose embryological term 'morula' derives from the Latin word for mulberry, is, before you know, an assembled aspect. She is your blood and bones transformed into rich gestures. She is a voice that echoes but isn't quite yours; a partial copy; a karyotype resemblance, one which resists and manipulates the prototype, being carried by its own synchronicity; a figure from the past and the ever-evolving, unpredictable, karmic future. The embodied genes, all twenty five thousand, from the twenty three pairs of chromosomes in the hundred-or-more trillion cells are randomly assorted, hybridised, watered down and contaminated by what is yours and not yours. So that what flowers strikes you at once suddenly and with tenderness in a manner that the Cuban writer Alejo Carpentier might have described as 'lo real maravilloso.' Or to put it another way, like the most terrifyingly beautiful living thing you have ever seen.

# JOHN CAREY

## *Ivan*

A Russian woodsman had most of his face scooped away like porridge from a bowl by a big brown bear. He was lucky enough, or not, to survive as an object of pity and horror to all but a few cosmetic surgeons who saw him as a challenge and a ticket to fame. They had to start from scratch and bite that gave them a blank canvas to work on, space for a masterpiece made of struts and impasto, a face that no genetic lottery could ever throw up, the face of a matinee idol or a mask of gravitas, paterfamilias of his people, the full incarnation of the Slavonic Soul.

The Socialist Realists among the surgeons were ousted after a coup and the Petersburg Spring left a new Master of the College of a humanist persuasion. He gave the woodsman Pushkin's eyebrows and the nose of Diaghilev. The shattered chin was shored up into a form worthy of bearing the beard of Tolstoy. The original eyes, left mostly undamaged, still held a darting, untrustful glance. He persuaded the subject to wear corrective lenses and train his gaze to a steady but sensitive repose, like the orbs of Shostakovitch.

Ivan's role as the new Homo Post-Sovieticus was a poor fit. He spurned the offers of every political party with a deep-rooted peasant suspicion and refused to tour North America with the surgeon, approving only a brief documentary film. Determined to face his demons, he joined a circus as an animal-wrangler and bear-whisperer, moving the brutes to tears with the full weight of his forgiveness. His only trip outside of Mother Russia was a visit to Poland to meet the family of a comely illusionist from Cracow, a colleague and friend and perhaps a little more.

This unfamiliar brush with tenderness and the monumental quality of his face filled Ivan with a need to mould his life into something it had never been. He learned to read more fluently, to play the balalaika. He replaced the rotting timbers of the village school at his own expense and gave comfort and alms to the poor, the sick and downtrodden.

But when a Patriarch proposed his village as a site of pilgrimage, Ivan felt the various elements of his sculpted lineage ripple and twist into the birthing of a new National Wisdom. All he allowed was the inclusion of his name in a modest Litany that would give no offence and be read only once a year, on his mother's birthday.

# SHADY COSGROVE

## *After school*

I was having sex for the first time in my life. Isobel's parents were working late and we were in her room—this crazy attic triangle with a window that looked straight into the forest. From her bed, I had this straight view of her walls, all layered with anti-globalisation posters and ticket stubs and notes like she was giving the finger to her neat-freak parents. Every bit of space was covered.

She unbuckled my belt. Her arm caught in her shirt and she made a face, which got us both laughing. The whole thing made me think of my little brother, Felix, who loved to strip off his t-shirt, inside out, so its round collar circled his forehead and the body of the shirt trailed behind him like a wig. Isobel was unclasping her bra and I was still thinking of my little brother. And in a moment like that you don't want to be thinking of your little brother—how he was playing soccer at home, how home felt so much further away than a fifteen-minute bus ride—so when Isobel's mouth landed on mine, I was grateful to be brought back. Her body was so immediate. So available. Whatever happened, I was ready: I'd been waiting for this.

'You okay?' she asked and I was thankful one of us knew what we were doing. I nodded. The mattress was a raft. She pulled me to the middle and rolled on top of me.

---

Her breasts were small and rounded with pale nipples; she drew my hands towards them so I could cup them in my palms. How could anyone mow the lawn, I wondered. How could you go grocery shopping or wait in line at the canteen when you could be doing this?

# *Visiting*

I saw my dead mother yesterday like she'd driven through time. She was stopped in city traffic, the car ahead of me. A bright blue 1970s Cortina 1600—squat, with bench seats and a side column shift. Her best friend from high school sat beside her. Both of them had long hair, pulled back with feathers. My mother was talking, one hand in the air, telling a joke or a story. Laughing. A piece of coral hung from the rear-view mirror between them.

My mother's right arm rested on the open window frame. I stared at her profile. She was wearing glasses, the same ones she wore in high school photos taken just before I was born. She reached down to the radio and began shifting the dial.

I thought of leaving my car, walking through the traffic lanes and knocking on the back door to be let in. I thought of pulling her from the car and refusing to let go, refusing to step aside even when horns blared from behind us. I was thinking of how tiny she'd been in that hospital bed—the steel rail, the too-small sheets—and how I'd climbed up beside her, afraid of crushing her. And then the light turned and the Cortina moved forward, changing lanes, rounding the corner towards the heart of the city before I could follow.

# MOYA COSTELLO

## *Australia: terra omnium*

Eucalyptus. Electric cars. Web designers, multimedia artists. Ferals, old hippies and refugees. Dentists in bow ties. Bocce and boule. Presidents of begonia and dahlia societies. Embroiderers Guild. Gay touring guides to Australia. Tennis players. Women's magazines. Vintage and classic car rallies. The RAA. Friends of the ABC. Friends of the Art Gallery. Members of MoMA. The Museum of Australian Painting. Black media. Chinese media. Arab media. Flying Fruit-Fly Circus. Stand-up comics. Trams. Poets and pop stars. Skate boarders, surfers and roller-bladers. Bicycle lanes. Conservation. Desalination. Anti-consumerism. Land claims. Native title. Feminism. Sugar cane, grape vines, canola, rice, olive groves, almonds, macadamia nuts, opium poppies, lavender, kauri forests, Huon pine, cannabis, magic mushrooms, truffles, Lebanese cucumbers, Vietnamese mint, bok choy, bush tomatoes, wattle seed, lemon myrtle. Body piercing. Shoemakers, tailors, dressmakers and milliners. Preschoolers: cultural production for the under-fives in TV, music, books, film, live performance. Festivals, music scholarships, prodigies. Boutique breweries. Biodynamics. Island resorts. Ferries. Angle parking. Roadside memorials. Cooking schools. Cenotaphs. Synagogues. Plaques. Nobel-Prize winners. Public sculpture. Permaculture. The CSIRO. Inventors. Architects. Publicly owned media. Aged-care and hospices. Wind farms. Recycling.

Rain forests. Alternative therapies. Female prime ministers. Aboriginal presidents of the republic. Sorry Day. Reconciliation. Platypus.

# *Slippery as a fish*

A time when life is slippery as a fish: a farmed rainbow trout that slips from your hands under tap water as you rinse it over the sink. You attend to the bright eye, the speckled coat, the flesh that will turn dusky pink, the slippage.

The natural mass extinctions of the past: the Late Ordovician, Late Devonian, Permian-Triassic, Late Triassic and Cretaceous-Tertiary, when, through asteroid or comet impact, volcanic eruption, sea-level fluctuation, climate change or global warming, many marine and land genera and species disappeared. Cod, haddock, herring, perch, swordfish disappear. You enter the fish market and in shock see fish piled high in mounds, triangular towers. This can't go on, you think, this mountain of fish in plentiful supply at a cheap price.

Once something solid and material, life becomes like the tap water running, something less than solid. Other things grow weighty, dense with mass: your heart's emotion, your head's thought; the weather; fortune, circumstance and synchronicity; desire; the movement of insects; the spirit of community; the falling of rain; the quality and availability of water.

An atomic bomb could go off. In the early nuclear age, Australians believed the trade winds would carry away radiation from nuclear war in the northern hemisphere. Defence against Radioactive Fallout on the Farm,...on the Suburban Dwelling, ... in the City's CBD. The equator as some kind of material barrier; all happening above, safe below. Hippies stowed themselves in the bush, far south, in Tasmania, to sit out an expected collapse. In the metropolis of Sydney, you looked at nightly TV weather reports to see wind directions, to know if fallout from a bomb dropped on the General Post Office in Martin Place, the middle of Sydney's CBD, would be carried out to you in the suburbs.

The polar ice caps melt; the sea level rises; the earth warms up. In the northern hemisphere, the counterpart of the hemisphere at the bottom of the world, far north, in Canada's high Arctic, the Inuit fall into thinning ice, lose their stores of meat which rots in the melt, are cold in refreezing igloos, find themselves on snowmobiles cut off from home by early-thawed ice turned to mud. The loss of ozone occurred beyond prediction. Nonlinear and surprising. Sudden, rapid, unexpected. Instruments were thought to be faulty; software wouldn't measure such a thing. Chlorofluorocarbons, halogen compounds, butyl and bromine, nitrogen oxides. Refrigeration, air conditioning, aerosols and solvents. Ozone as the muslin curtain, the bubble, the balloon, the membrane. Ultraviolet radiation strikes like Star Wars, some intergalactic fantasy. Illness, deaths, extinctions, solid, fully rounded phenomena, dropping with the dead weight of lead balls into a pool of water. Cataracts, melanomas, immune system suppression through the expansion of decay, the infiltration of poison. You could get a malignant melanoma. Oil could stop flowing. The age of fossil fuels ends; the twenty-first century,

40

third millennium, one of disintegration. The age of renewable energy, wind and sun, photovoltaic cells, hydrogen and methane begins. All drinking water could be polluted. Biological or germ warfare could get you. Seed companies create seed infertile and stillborn, producing only once, so you have to buy more. Petrochemical companies acquire seed companies, enter biotech industries, reaping pesticide-dependent crops. Cosmos, Queen Anne's lace, marigolds, basil, pumpkin, tomato still reproduce themselves out of the compost like friends returning, resilient, defiant in good measure. You discover them, like lighting upon a star. They appear, sprouted; you watch, they develop. A simple meal, drink or medication could poison you. You could get heart disease. Allergies are de rigueur, coutured, auteured: gluten, sugar, dairy, hormone-infested meat, the solanum family, wine both red and white, histamines, MSG, salt, engineered genes, fat, high heat, carbohydrates.

A meteor could crash into earth. You could crash in a plane. The limb of a tree, hail from the sky could crash your car with you in it. Your workplace could blow up. You could be burgled. You could be mugged. You could become a bully. Bullying, and personal and corporate treachery, are strategies to deal with a fear-filled universe. But you decide on the value of the moment, no longer on the future. And you decide on 'radical politeness', civility, courtesy to fellow human beings—R-E-S-P-E-C-T in absentia—as grassroots political activity, at a time of late capitalism: the ruthlessly competitive, the disregarding, the selective securing of privilege, the abusive, the ascription of fanaticism to religion but never to money markets and the stock exchange.

Australia as large land mass surrounded by water: an island continent. Tectonic plates make for the ordering and labelling of continents—cans on the shelves, files in the cabinet. Australia and India together on the same piece of lithic crust. Oceania, beautifully named, a distinct part of the world, collects under its rubric Southeast Asia, Australia, New Zealand and the islands of the Pacific. We align with Asia, Asia-Pacific and the Pacific Rim, as a sharp, smart, uptown, together economic move. Beijing, Tokyo, Seoul, Hong Kong, Singapore, Sydney. Ocean currents, fringing seas, islands, island groups and coral outcrops. The watery part of the world, the Pacific holding more water than all other oceans combined, covering the deepest and the lowest planet's place, extending through tropics to the Arctic and Antarctic. The new world. Capital, markets and commodities; cheap labour and sweatshops; great wealth and impoverishment.

Present in the Phanerozoic Aeon, the Cenozoic Era, the Quaternary Period, the Holocene Epoch, are the most exotic and ordinary, effective and efficient powers of destruction.

# *Travelling (east–west)*

The terraced rice fields are half-mouths shoved forward. Graded palazzo steps for dancing down in style. Green, brown and black simulate earth far afield.

A sarong, a feathered layer of the body.

The staple of bread becomes holy with heat.

Saffron, the colour of an Indian song, Bindu, the red spot, my pinprick, my jeweled crown. I'd be a centrifuge wearing it in the streets of Manly. My core blood, a passage of light, a portal to ... A mark of wisdom. A seer in her shawl telling fortunes.

The terracottas in Chandigarh Museum are spotlit heads of women encased in glass. They smile silently to themselves. Their curved lips carry inscrutable expressions. Time and place are nothing to them. They have survived centuries in their serenity. They will outlive the museum. Their cool superiority breathes over the innocent spectator.

A skull cap. A tea-cosy for my addled brain.

Chador. A walking curtain.

Mushroom houses of Goreme. Pixie homes.

The Bosporus. A water highway.

'*Thalassa, thalassa.*' The sea, the sea.

Missed the boat to the mainland.

Cafés catering to men. Their worry beads. With hats and moustaches, playing cards and small chalkboards for scoring.

Delphi is set-designer's envy: a cliff face, vast sky, a low valley.

The Cycladic sculptures are creamy white. Thin limbs are plasticine rolled to smoothness in child's play. These small moderns are animated. The harpist from Keros is in a Wishbone chair; the figurine's got a Modigliani head! Ha!

Honey in cake, in a fried pasty. A mud wall subsides.

Remains of temples far above.

Bread rings with sesame seeds to buy off street hawkers.

I keep guidebooks in my pack. I'm disposing of them one by one.

Giving lollies in change. It's an anarchic economy. *Commedia dell'arte.*

The ghosts have left the Colosseum in the middle of cars.

Candy was strung under lights in a market stall in the Plaza Nuovo. The staff of life. Its excess?

Christmas, and I wasn't homesick. Unexpected. Being away from home is just an inconvenience.

In Rome, a room overlooking terracotta tiles of rooftops, a bell tower. Green shutters on my window. My book is *A Room with a View.*

Marble and the Renaissance. Something becoming.

A wedding in Greece. A funeral gondola in Venice.

A Capri morning of cliffs and water.

In the railway station café, I take croissant after croissant from a plate covered in a plastic dome, as if I didn't have to pay.

*Pommes frites*: small person in hand-knitted beret with pompom. Someone famous I'd like to know. A friend who's always entertaining.

Morning bread and milk coffee.

In the Musée Rodin I can see a child in the park outside. She's wrapped from head to toe against the cold. Plays hide and seek around an old-man tree. She catches the ball trailing along the wet gravel path. And look, mothers, nannies, au pairs. Here inside the light from large windows, mirrors and chandeliers illuminates all. The surfaces of Rodin's sculptures are shiny and muscular. Warmth oozes through the rooms. I wander from the sinuous figures to rest somewhere. In every half turn in the circular rooms I see the park. A muscular back is taut over a woman. I'm drowsy with heat, light and love.

French perfume. Liquid gold. Sometimes I could trade in amber. Heat becomes vapour. Afternoon sun.

The Max Ernsts are hilarious. They're repulsive. To have been Max Ernst.

*Brillo Box*. A grocery-store shelf. Compulsion masquerading as choice. I stop and I think: I'm miniaturised before this Minotaur.

The palace of Louis XIV. Tell me: how all those corridors could be home?

Pernod and water. A cloudy transubstantiation.

18f menu and *price fixe*. A fortune teller's meal. I like the comfort of rules.

French windows are my heart. Senses wide open. Memory lies down like a rug. Tea or drinks. Friends, music and conversation. The colour of the sky. The temperature of the air. The world enters into a limited space and fits.

The Seine. Have a river if you can't have a harbour. The names call themselves into existence. An echo.

I'm fed on names: Poissonnerie, Boulanger, Herboristerie. Sometimes I could digest through my eyes.

The skeleton of Gaudi's cathedral. Wind blows through its bones. Where is its skin? Outer covering? Coat of comfort?

Tudor housing. The childhood boxes of cardboard imagined to be mansions.

A hotel room is not a home.

Today I am heading to the museums.

The tour bus didn't wait for me. I took another path.

# ANNA COUANI

## *The old manuscript*

Looking back at an old manuscript. Broken, like pieces of a china cup. But never in one piece to begin with. I think of pieces of white porcelain, fragile segments, and of the sculpture at Sculpture by the Sea called 11:11.[1] Frosted glass columns, triangular with spirals etched on them.

Meant by the artist to represent a gateway, the gateway represented by those numbers. For her this has a cosmic connection and some believe that all of us who notice 11:11 on digital time-pieces are ready to receive our spiritual guardians.

My manuscript was disrupted by another manuscript that had to be written. Now the old manuscript comes back to haunt me. I see the people in it, shadows from Surry Hills in the 60's. Shadowy figures. My teenage years were spent being watched. Older housewives reporting to my parents. Migrant bachelors signalling to me from first-storey windows, following me into town.

The photo of the 11:11 sculpture. There are no shadows and no reflections, no contrast. The frosty pillars with the blue-green sea behind them, and the pale yellow sandstone pebbles. Naples yellow. The glass melts into its background. So beautiful, but is it the artwork or the photo.

'I remember you as a teenager,' he said, the publisher guy, 'at the Ban the Bomb marches. Walking down Bayswater Road to The Stadium.' Later, his warehouse was burned down.

I was aware, like a self-conscious teenager, of being watched. But now, I realise, of course we were all being watched.

A friend shows me a massive tome—the ASIO records of just one Greek–Australian journalist. Every meeting, every interaction documented. There we were, dancing the Cha Cha Cha at the Greek Atlas Club and suspected of plotting the downfall of the Australian political system.

Researching the 11:11 phenomenon, I come across the US anarchist Kerry Thornley, master of conspiracy theories, some of them possible. Thornley thought that Lee Harvey Oswald had been a CIA operative looking for Communist sympathisers in the US armed forces.

The old manuscript already found spies in the Greek community. A community split in half by politics. The manuscript searches for a path through the miasma of fiction, delusion and biography. Tracking down the truth. I was there, but what was it I was seeing?

[1] 11:11 sculpture is by Alison Lee Cousland

# CHARLES D'ANASTASI

## *Madame Bovary*

Behind each solitary reader: a wall with two windows, city
noises, night. What cuts across during the silence, while one voice
reads, and another one follows, as the list of poets is worked
through, is the sound of the horses' hoofs on the tarmac, and the
jingle of harnesses; noises that seem to have mesmerised these
condemned creatures to follow the same route, past the mess of
shops, restaurants, churches and this room's two windows.

Some of the poet's words escape me. The horses' hoofs have
weakened all the other sounds and silences inside the room, but
blend naturally with the traffic and the faded night voices of
the streets. I think of a woman and a man, the drawn curtains
of their carriage, their snatched hours, their soul—an anxious
clock in disarray, the clacking sound of the horses' hoofs. You'd
think surely someone else in this room would stir to the rhythm
of ruination in that long-discarded book. Yet no one appears to
have noticed anything unusual. A woman gentles a hand to her
throat, raises a glass of wine to her lips. Someone drags a chair,
leaves the room. Ritual applause follows the calling of another
poet's name.

I dislodge easily from the benevolence of this room, and wait
to fall under the inevitable spell—the reapproaching sound of

the horses' hoofs, the lovers in their abandonment, crazed by the weightlessness of their despair, unable to leave the eternal carriage of their life, as it hurtles aimlessly like a piece of space debris, past stars, and long-period comets, stripped down by repeated surgery of the night.

# MICHAEL FARRELL

## *The story of what's inside the heart*

When someone's going to kill you, love you, they like to know what's inside you. I feel like that too and_don't even know you. I came out of the bush, I put my hand in the wound in your side (wanting to know what was there). It wasn't poetry. No 'story' either: the story was inside the story. The love was defined in the love; and, looking in—at the ink *in* the ink—I saw the language that was in language. The Renaissance In The Renaissance. And it was all there. It was the wait inside the wait—it was the happening *inside* the happening. Even Jesus_when we opened him up was *full*—of Jesus! That was the case of the case for many of us, and not so long_in the not so long ago. The hurt's still felt inside the hurt. The names are still all inside the names. Not forgetting the crows inside the cross inside the cross inside the crows ... Everyone wants to know what it means. To fill their knowing with knowing; to feel the blood inside their blood. Listen to the song in and of_the song. I came out of the radio_and was a radio. The purity of radio was other to the purity of song-birds—the birds that flew into_and out of being birds. Inside the difference, difference, they sang; inside the same, the same. In every country, they found that country. Open him up! There were questions inside questions; worries coiled in worries. He's going into the clock: there's a clock there, and it chimes. It ticks! It lies! Lies that have no inside—or outside. Lies that are told

53

by no one, to no one ... aren't told at all. They're not *narrated*. According to the face, it was in honey; the honey and the face were one, but Jack said ... It's for you: you see in what you see. Cubes of meat, cut ever smaller. Glasses of coke, going on forever. 'Come into the house. Come into the house.' See the iron iron iron ... There was a self-made spice rack. A guitar, an infinitely alcoholic guitar. When the stars pierce you, when you feel the heart beating in (the heart of) your heart (the stars that are in the stars, the imploding moonlight), when you open yourself up and are all heart, all blood opening, all you, and_no one knows. They're more concerned with their pockets: full of pockets. Their concern's so concerned, so concerning. Yeah, and there's so much style in style, it's the only thing to eat; spoon by spoon, heart by mouse by_little green die ... with a skull on it instead of a five. When you throw it you know_your I's still alive. Your alive's still alive.

# ADAM FORD

## *Sequel*

The aliens and cowboys put aside their cultural differences and work together toward a mutually beneficial future. They forgive each other the violence of their first encounters and forge a lasting alliance based on empathy, compassion and co-operation. Laser cannons are retrofitted to become powerplants. Colt revolvers are melted down and turned into hammers and nails. The aliens take the cowboys to the Moon, to Jupiter, to HD 33564 b. They teach the cowboys the names of these places in their own alien language, inhuman syllables ghosting out over methane seas and echoing back from mountains of pure cobalt. The cowboys teach the aliens to ride, their pseudopods coupled underneath their mounts' bellies like living stirrups. They take them out to the prairie and teach them to sing 'Arizona Killer' and 'Red River Valley', their voices rising to meet the halo that circles the desert moon. Cowboys round up proto-comets in the Oort Cloud. Aliens teleport runaway steers back home. Moon dust gathers on bootheels. Tobacco juice stains scaly green chins. The aliens start wearing spurs, holsters, stetsons. The cowboys start wearing bubble helmets, space-suits, jetpacks. Soon it's impossible to tell the difference between an alien cowboy and a cowboy alien, and then there's no telling the cowboys from the aliens or the aliens from the cowboys at all.

# KERI GLASTONBURY

## *New Delhi: for Sophea Learner*

Flânerie transposed through the mud and cow shit at the vege-
table markets after rain. Backward angels don't fear to tread
but Def. Col. residents rarely cross. The huge black bullock at
the intersection is one way to slow traffic, pedestrians walking
on the road, another. Like a bicycle rickshaw driver in the heat
I've learnt not to apply my thresholds to others. You lie on the
bed fatigued, embodying the expatriate dialectic: transnational
buzz meets an almost vampiric torpor. I see none of the sights,
not even a Moghul ruin (neither of us particularly motivated)
and prefer the residential interstices. Kaustubh makes dhal in a
pressure cooker and works as an open-source programmer. He's
affectionate and sweet and gives hugs like an indymedia kid. We
could be on a rooftop in Enmore: the fold-up bike parked at the
door; the electric car plugged in at the socket; the pet rescue cats.
The X and Y generations are imprinted like chromosomes, the
transfer of files a slow pirating.

# *Shanghai baby: for Christen Cornell*

The city does and undoes the vestige of oriental romance, there's girl-most-likely meets the reality of the locals playing mah-jong in a room at the bottom of the stairs. No one seems to really get out much, they're more likely to just yell across to each other. You start to recognise dresses hanging out on the street, which have a certain intimate animus. It's a sense of neighbourhood you associate with Sesame Street, not the future of China–Australia relations: *that's when good neighbours become good friends.* The exact type of friendship is the (then) Prime Minister's stroke of genius. I'm loathe to comment after only eleven days, though Barthes' diaries are published after a similarly short trip he took in the 70s. He found Mao's China boring, but perhaps he was thinking more about the naivety of French intellectuals in solidarity getting only bad airline food, ping-pong and State opera. The aesthete in him wanted to be back in Japan. Sure, the old folk are Dirty Dancing to a tape recorder on the back of a truck in Fuxing Park, but it's beyond semiotic fetish in the retro Hong Kong diner where the emo kids hang out.

# MONICA GOLDBERG

## *The stranger from Skierniewicza*

*Reason is immortal. All else is mortal.* Pythagoras

I watch her drinking vodka behind a piano stool at the May Rock Festival in Skierniewicza. It's my third visit to Poland and I am still scared. Scared of her chords and her intervals. Afraid that I belong here. She knows the piano strings which pull the old ghetto into focus. She knows how to compress and create time. She flies me past the peeling stars. Through the mausoleum of the holy man and past the exact shop where we once owned our grocery store. We take our seats at the festival and wait for the tones and the vowels. We wait to be transformed and for the concert to begin. We discuss Pythagoras and his theory on hammers. We exchange stories in Russian, Yiddish, Chinese, Spanish and all languages of the world. We talk about the spacing of the spheres and her march to Rawa Mazowiecka. We invent ways to quieten her trembling. The performance starts with a piano in C major then into D minor. The notes are crisp but the air still smells of sewer and soup. She tells me that all lives are fictional. True or not, I will never know.

# ERIN GOUGH

## *William Shatner vows to save the Great Basin Pocket Mouse*

It rained all night. It was always raining in Vancouver. Stella spread the newspapers out on Maxime's mattress.

'I don't believe it!' she called in outrage to Maxime, who was standing at the stove on the other side of the room, making instant mashed potato, pretending to listen. 'It says here: *William Shatner vows to save the Great Basin Pocket Mouse.*'

Maxime made her instant mashed potato in an enormous second-hand wok designed for an industrial kitchen, a weighty grease-stained thing that she kept on one of ten butcher hooks that hung above her bench top. Regarding the necessity of woks for the purposes of instant mashed potato preparation, there had already been a conversation.

'Isn't the idea that you just add water? Can't you do it in a bowl?'

And Maxime had said, 'What would you know about it? Are you a Canadian now? Are you an expert in the national cuisine?'

Her point being that instant mashed potato was a Canadian invention. Her point being that Stella knew this.

Canadian-versus-Australian Inventions was a game they played regularly as part of the great entanglement of their breath and bodies; a low, passion-blurred recitation as their mouths pressed against each other's flesh.

'Washing machine,' Maxime would mumble for Canada, rolling slick and sweat-lipped to mark the imaginary tally board on Stella's thigh with a single clip-nailed finger.

'Penicillin,' Stella would reply for Australia, limb-locked and urgent.

'Clothes zipper. Dental mirror.'

'Two-stroke lawnmower. Black box flight recorder.'

'Trivial Pursuit.' Heaving.

'Ute.' Panting.

'Anti-*aah*-gravity suit.'

Stella heard a rhythmic banging from the kitchen; Maxime was beating the potato mixture with a fork.

'I don't see the problem with William Shatner wanting to save houses,' Maxime said.

'Not houses: *mouses*,' said Stella. 'They've got nothing to do with him. He's a television actor.'

'He's a personality,' said Maxime, studying with satisfaction the stiff white peaks that rose up from the wok. 'And I think you'll find it's *mice*.'

# GREGORY A GOULD

## *The story of the thin red book that sits on the bookshelf*

It goes like this: you were living in China at the time. With a young American student. A kind young American student who believed in God. And good manners. And the right to carry a gun. The book was his. But you loved it. You said he only bought it because a teacher had made him. He didn't even like it. So you took it. Just like that. Last day in that place. You put the book in your bag. Put your bag in a cab. Shook the kind young American's hand and said: thanks, this has been swell. Then. You left. Got on a plane. Came home. Put that thin red book on the bookshelf. Called it your own. A book I've never read. But a story I know so well.

# PHILIP HAMMIAL

## *Gold*

Hiawatha's Hawaiian executor chooses to disregard the antics
of Zania Bryce who, having just rushed into the Café Zamboco
to deliver a slap to the face of her suitor, the elegant immigrant
Paco Rojas, is now sitting on a curb waiting for the Money Men
to cruise slowly by in a black Cadillac. She knows that one of
them will open a door & kick out a corpse that will land at her
feet, a body worth its weight in gold if only she can manage to
drag it into the Body Shop just a few doors down from the Café
Zamboco, a task for which she'd like to enlist the services of
Paco, but he of course will refuse (he always does) not wanting
to soil his elegant immigrant's hands (hence the slap on the face)
& so she has no recourse but to approach with a great show of
humility Hiawatha's Hawaiian executor who, beneath the hard
exterior, is a man of compassion. It's a struggle, but between
them they manage to drag the corpse down the footpath & into
the Body Shop where, as expected, it's found to be worth its
weight in gold.

# *Milk*

'Sailors on cattle. And they don't have saddles. What's the world coming to?' 'It's coming to the time, & very soon, when everything will be milked for all it's worth —sailors & cattle, ships & seas ...'

# Tony's museum

Tony has opened a museum of madness. He's persuaded the administrators to lease one of the rooms in the basement of the Museum of Natural History—a huge, high-ceilinged room in which the displays—in glass cases & cabinets—are arranged in the form of a maze. In these cases & cabinets are objects, strange, often sinister-looking objects that Tony has brought back from his many forays into that place called *madness*. There are also maps, charts, drawings & journals, all with 'scientific' explanations neatly printed on white cards in a Gothic script. In one of the dead ends of the maze, behind a thick black velvet curtain, the museum visitor encounters a mob of tiny people, not dwarves, but tiny people about two feet high. They ask the visitor for an arm which, if given, will be viciously fought over, the visitor lucky to get it back again. And the admission price—only $1.50, which may explain why there are hundreds of people waiting to get in, a line that extends down a long corridor, up a flight of stairs to the entrance foyer, out into the weather—it's pouring buckets—& down the footpath (a sea of umbrellas) to the end of the block.

# *Traps*

Article 12 expressly forbids the digging of traps in public gardens. Article 13, in apparent contradiction to 12, declares that all traps in public gardens must be camouflaged with the leaves of banyan trees, oak leaves never, under any circumstances, to be used for this purpose. Article 14, in apparent contradiction to 12 & 13, states that everyone, without exception, who has fallen into an oak leaf-covered trap in any public garden in the month of May is required to attend a banquet at the Town Hall on June 1, a banquet presided over by the mayor who at this solemn occasion will present keys to the city to the May trapees.

# STU HATTON

## *meds*

Piercing blister foil with thumbnail. Those who call them meds generally those who take them (target group). As if a pill might mainstream you. Conditioned air.

Body became a fist, clenched. Having no designated evacuation assembly point. If resistance alone is real. Tension of the oral.

Pharmaceutical packaging design says what about what? Bring colour. Cropped Riviera panorama. Starter pack (like life is a series of hobbies).

Had never been held by a cloud before. Perennial tremor. A little blur. Doesn't fit in the eye.

The white coats only prepared to discuss rituals of personal sanitation in light of the overarching norm. They think they own white light. Smudge that. Gaze predicated on someone's plotline of progress.

In need of new plottings, new flows. Medicated for fear of the phone. There is something necromantic. Hi, I'm fine.

Recalibrating one's categories of silence. Silence can mean anything but. Slight decoherence. Are you feeling?

Late needs, late needers. Consider the implications of 'appetite alterant'. Of appetite. What is burnt to milk a glow.

Entering that hummingbird space. Getting to know those stranded outside the fifteenth wall. Wet with voices. Not possessing that movement.

Agonists, all. Neurotransmitter pool. Disinhibitor set him on a biting spree. The two photos show him before and after science.

Shipped or funnelled back to consensus reality. Homecoming of sorts, arms open like clouds. A bath of wool. How to be welcome.

# *refuse*

A day under repair. Unable to stand after meditating (my foot dead as a book). Trying to type but the window was ghosted. Coming down with something: perhaps a poem. My turn to call? Half-life: transactions blur between us; signal fray. Go through phases, moods, like some old moon. Naming will not keep pace. Downloading Derrida. I looked the instant it ticked over. Have a tic about time. Distraction blizzards. Dwelling in the centre of your palm. You've lost me. Cherry-fingers blemish the page. A guilt that grows back. Comedown. Log out, log back in again. Need to work back late, keep watch till dawn. As markets cloud. Remove nothing from the scene of the theft. Where dying is a slowness. Emissions. Heavy myself with. Punjabi pop music strays from another apartment, as if dappling me with colour. I wasn't quite full. Was deleting old songs. The crouched hand of love (from a song of Creeley's). New window. Wheeling towards stories of failures. Driver error. Lab rats in lab coats? They were subtitles for a different film altogether. Photograph these powers of persuasion. But does he look happy to you? Wasting berserker-bots in Timezone. Heroic dopamine leak. Doctor suggests closing both eyes. Hyperrealism of high definition. Have fun with it? Sad snaps. Exit the bed via the usual exit. Bivouac: *noun*; a military encampment made with tents or improvised shelters, without protection from enemy fire. Have overslept. Just one more snooze

---

69

before we assemble. Another day speechless, the mouth a lock. Away from the meat. Touch of the air, air of the touch. Refused endings. Everything's not you in one sense, but in another: come home. Swim your body for the first time. Untie these roads and lift them from you.

# CAROL JENKINS

## *An illustrated history of the bicycle*

for Tani Ruckle

### Origins of the domestic bicycle

The domestic bicycle, as we now know it, is descended from the wild Cyclops, a free-ranging species originating in Eastern Europe during the Paleolithic period. The Cyclops was a herd animal, sturdier and shorter than the modern bicycle, with upright, hirsute horns. The Cyclops spread quickly through an innovative symbiotic strategy which some archaeologists believe may have occurred before its widespread domestication. Its modern descendant, the bicycle, has kept going, and now has colonised nearly every ecological niche in the planet.

### Early cyclops in cave art

A recent study of the distribution of bicycle DNA shows that bicycles radiated out from the grasslands and wooded fields of Eastern Europe along primitive lanes and pathways. By the late Neolithic period they had reached Southern France. Cave paintings of herds of Cyclops can be seen at Grotte du Placard, Chauvet Cave and Gargas, where it is suggested that herds or pelotons of wild Cyclops would undertake an annual migration around what is now the south of France. There may be some race memory for migration which gave rise to the Tour de France.

---

**The bicycle as a food source?**

Like its modern counterpart the wild Cyclops appears to have been a particularly unpalatable animal, tough, with a nearly metallic taste to the flesh. It seems it was never hunted for food, though later, once domesticated, herds were hunted for sport, and single bicycles taken for spare parts.

**Domestication of the bicycle**

One theory is that wild Cyclops were domesticated by *Homo cyclopsis*, who at dawn lured them into traps set out with brightly coloured fabric, caffeinated drinks and tool kits, which are highly prized by all Cyclop species. Archaeological digs at Petrovka in the Ural Mountains have found something thought to have been chariot graves but with bicycle wheels and handle bones, along with weapons and human skeletal remains. This is the earliest evidence of a domesticated bicycle. Once tamed, bicycles could be fitted with brakes and leather seats, and used as transport, though often, it seems, the animals wearied of the whole business and would slink off and vanish. As bicycles were important status symbols, a lost bicycle was often considered a tragedy. The moving song cycle *Lament for Cycles Past*, still sung in remote villages in Kazakastan, is believed to be from the Botai culture of 3500–3000 BCE.

**Alternative theory of domestication**

The other more controversial theory is that the Cyclops species originally set out to lure in early man—the so-called *Homo cyclopsis*—setting out tool kits, caffeinated drinks and brightly coloured fabrics, which the *H. cyclopsis* find nearly impossible to ignore. Once it had lured its human in for a ride,[1] the early bicycle would deliberately nip the calves and ankles of its rider with its sharp lower teeth infecting it with the cyclopsis virus. It is thought the speed at which bicycles spread was due in part to the spread of the cyclopsis virus through the *H. cyclopsis*'s social network.

Some scientists suggest this bicycle/human relationship was a form of symbiosis, though others take a view it should be considered a form of parasitism. This infection and subsequent behavioural change is thought to have a similar mechanism to that seen in mice infected with toxoplasmosis virus, which sets up risky behavioural patterns in the infected mice that render them susceptible. Once infected, mice frequently fail to take cover when a cat appears and are quickly caught. Modern humans infected with the cyclopsis virus will linger over bicycling magazines, visit cycle shops and participate in long discussions about the Tour de France.

### Is the bicycle still capable of independent movement?

The human domestication of the bicycle or, as the alternative hypothesis would have it, the bicycles' domestication of humans, has made the bicycle all but lame, and dependent on humans to provide it with the caloric input essential to movement. There is evidence to suggest that modern bicycles retain vestigial mobility due to the high disappearance rate of unchained bicycles, traditionally attributed to theft. Modern bicycles may appear to be solitary but have a clandestine and complex social hierarchy; once they herd together on the road into their social peloton they can be fiercely territorial. Riders should be aware that though domesticated now for millennia, a bicycle's primitive urge to graze on open grasslands or road verges can resurface, unseating the inattentive rider.

[1] Linguists theorise this may be the origin of the expression 'taken for a ride'.

# Co-evolution

The first eggs ever laid were covered in a fine pelt of nutrient fuzz which grew out of the many pores in the shells. The pelt kept the egg warm and acted as camouflage, allowing the Egg Layer to leave the egg to its own devices. The animal within the furred shell, known as an Eggling, would wind in the nutrient fuzz, eating it with a distinct pattern that identified both the animal and when it would emerge. This meant the Egg Layer could keep a watchful eye on its progress. Some of the more sophisticated Egglings invented a rudimentary alphabet, writing their name, invariably with the suffix, or prefix, 'Egg'.

The trouble with this evolutionary grand-standing was it taught egg-collecting species how to read, putting the eggs at greater risk. Those Egg Layers and Egglings that did not quickly adapt to readers, and shed the hair with its overt declaration of edible contents, became extinct. Evidence for this hirsute history can been seen in modern eggs which are covered with vestigial microscopic pores. If you examine them closely you will sometimes find the word 'egg' is still faintly patterned into the shell.

# JO LANGDON

## *Pause*

In primary school I started to tell stories about our dad, and my brother let me.

I would tell the kids that our old man flew planes, or built them. Bolted together steel wings and cut out rows of little windows that would fill with sky. Or that he was a glassmaker who assembled whole chandeliers that hung in grand houses from ceilings that looked like wedding cake. Or I said he worked on a squid boat, one of those lights swollen on the night horizon. Or that he was a policeman and carried a gun at his hip and another in his boot. Or that he beat our mum. Swung whiskey bottles against the wall so glass exploded and showered down onto the tiles. Threw his shoes at us, or made us drink bleach or piss.

And then sometimes I'd wait for him in the afternoons, pretending I wasn't. Sometimes Kip would come and crouch down beside me in the driveway, and we'd break quartz pieces with heavier stones and believe in diamonds. One day we found our dad's hammer and it made the task quicker. We spent an afternoon pretending rocks were gems, splitting bits of blue gravel in half to see the pale gold vein running through them.

In high school I said nothing but ate away my fingernails remembering him, but by then he'd been gone years. Walking home from school I'd curl my fingers into my palm so Kip wouldn't see the blood crust that edged each of my bitten-off nails.

Later, in our Melbourne house, I'd sometimes bring him up again. Knifing a grid into a mango cheek I'd pause and say, it could be that he went North, fruit-picking.

Or I'd see him boxing up bananas to pack off in trucks, and finding a tree frog. Peeling it away from the fruit and almost shivering at the damp adhesion of its green feet to his skin.

Or pearling, someplace like Broome. My warped toaster reflection would smile absently at Kip's as I loaded the bread.

Could be a fucking astronaut, Kip would say quietly, and lick his lips. I'd shut up then, saying nothing but letting every door I put between us slam shut loudly so that the house walls shook.

Our dad would arrive on Fridays, and how long he stayed would depend on the sounds we heard in the night, the weight of his boots on the floorboards, or how Mum's face looked in the morning. At breakfast we ate cornflakes with sugar and no milk. My brother would watch the same huntsman that had pock-marked the ceiling for weeks, and that he'd named Bruce Wayne. I'd watch our dad long enough for him to tell me to cut it out.

When it rained, Kip and I brought in snails and fed them warm milk. They threaded silver maps across the floor, atlases that remained on the blue kitchen tiles long after we returned them to the wet garden path bricks. I would tell my brother how, if our dad saw the snails in the house, he would step on them hard, and Kip would tell me to just shut up.

Once we watched our parents from the window, kissing outside and our dad holding Mum softly by the shoulders until she pulled away, cupping a hand to her nose as if to catch a sneeze. She's crying, dickhead, Kip said when I spoke, and pulled the curtains together so I couldn't look again.

On the afternoons his ute arrived we'd pitch ourselves at him before the seatbelt had been unclipped or the engine cut, skidding across the split vinyl of the seats. Mum would stand away some distance but near enough to watch how our easy intimacy frightened him.

Sometimes he stayed the weekend, others he left that same night, tyres chewing through the gravel once we were put to bed. Either way we would look for traces of him after, something tactile and true. Usually the best we could find was an emptied coffee mug forgotten on the verandah, or a ring of sticky whiskey on the bench. Other times there might be a throwaway razor. A Gillette Blue Blade, its edges dulled with cut whiskers and the fatty residue of soap. Once I souvenired a box of matches from his glove compartment and we lit them one by one. Striking them away from us like he'd taught, watching the flame edge down the splintery strip to our fingertips, moving like a bright orange centipede. After they were all burned out we fitted them back in their box, sliding the lid over and sealing it shut like a little cardboard coffin.

BANANAS

# KENT MacCARTER

## *Light foxing*

You hound ½ of an indefensibly slow conversation between air and hairdos of a paperback or many slatternly bodice rippers...and your chitchat is remarkably similar to an apple's; when it's cut, how it browns, amazing eyes, chemistry's whim puffing off dust from its box of redox reactions like trains modelled in HO scale and found wedged deep in garages, timid operas though both are. They've lost their plastic freight loads between the juice of a paragraph and codas of reddish-brown to yellowish-brown moisture seeping in, most noticeably on endpapers which cannot cease their square-dancing steps with charts or illustrations vying for Miss Congeniality. At best. There's growing consensus on culprits here; how they're fungal or mineral or both in origin—lighter, concentric polka dots which contend for beatification by iron although fungus may still play a role, as it plays on aged manchego abandoned to brood and waterlog in humid environments; warm, say, like all of Suriname. To use a dehumidifier is a relatively inexpensive solution to this centuries-old flummoxing: what portends this discolouration? How its acid infection is rather like a malarial outbreak on those critical chapters which machete their heroines through deep, darkest jungles, lugging the bulk of a novel along like a passenger train carving its plotline through topography, shrubs of literacy that rate in rural Wyoming.

# CLARE McHUGH

## *Briefly*

Short? I'll give you short. I've had a lifetime of Short. Let's not euphemise—micro, mini, petite, regular-serve—it's all short.

But what kind of Short did you want? A short sentence?

It's yours.

Are you really ready for Short? Short shrift. Short changed. Short odds. Caught short.

Don't think you can arrive at it by falling short: by thinking it is merely less than full serve. A sandwich short of a picnic.

Short is not easier. It takes time. More goes into making less.

Philosophers understand. Pascal apologised for a long letter. Didn't have time to write a brief one.

Builders do not understand. All those mirrors in bathrooms and public toilets. Short means scraping to see your forehead—in your own home.

Only once did I order Short: a custom-made sofa. I asked for the legs to be shortened to match my own. More comfortable. The saleswoman looked doubtful. Thought it would ruin the lines. Aesthetics. She went to fetch the catalogue while I pondered Aesthetics and the line of my back, ruined from years of stretching, reaching, legs left swinging.

Short is Brevity: soul of wit. Economy: the opposite of glutenous, gluttonous excess. Implies judicious. Chosen.

Short is essence.

A Short History of Australia, of sheep husbandry, of almost anything will invariably be the most important, densely-packed, don't-leave-home-without-it bits.

But don't be fooled. Some people think short is sweet. Even a little comic. It can bring out the urge to pat, protect, laugh, to goo and gaa. Sensible people—sometimes with large ears or noses, who would never strike up conversation with: 'You're bald, aren't you?'—think nothing of remarking on short. Its cuteness, its pattability. Then pause for your laughter.

Cute can be disarming. But beware who is disarmed.

Short is dangerous, especially when underestimated.

Short black means strong. Not to be messed with. A shot of something dark and powerful. It can keep you up long into the night.

Short fuse: a lot, coming out of a small space, with little time. Run for your life.

Short and punchy: has impact but don't turn your back—there might be a surprise. It sneaks up on you because you were expecting something more ... something more substantial.

You let down your guard, didn't you?

Like a short life. Was that it ...?

Is there any more?

If you'd known it was going to be so short ...

# ALYSON MILLER

## *Impossible*

On a night when the universe is a box of pinpricks, the highway is teeming with alien lights under skies that seem to whisper of astronauts & starbursts that will burn your mind. But it's not a sacrilege to say that some things are impossible, no matter how hard you look at the moon or use the existence of dinosaurs as an example of how unreal the real can be. Perhaps the unattainable is only a trick of the cosmos or maybe of perspective, in the same way that the angle of my camera suggested you could hold the sun & then eat it whole. Unnoticed for years, you stole pages from books fat full of words, ripping moments from stories in the hope they could be planted elsewhere & create infinite circles of telling. As a child, you ran between trees with stick swords & a cardboard helmet, battling monsters from nowhere that ghosted your home and the silence of the gum trees, simply because you believed you could. The mystery of these things, like the mind of a fish, the weight of the air, the making of Easter eggs & the loss of self in sleep & orgasm, make you wonder how atoms & gravity manage to keep us from falling apart.

# CARA MUNRO

## *An arrangement*

From our little rooftop home, Sonia is set to jump.

Locked in the tin-doored bathroom, the high window pasted over with a piece of torn newspaper. The news today is Anesh came round this afternoon and demanded that she marry him. Across the rooftops and into the ears of small, kite-flying boys and water-carrying girls, he shouted that she had led him on, flirted with him. Deceived him into thinking that she was in love. He shouted that he had told his family, and she was coming with him this afternoon.

And she had shouted back across the rooftop. That he was crazy. A possessive monster. That she would sooner death carry her away than him. And then he had slapped her and she had taken the red plastic washing bucket and broken it against the side of his face. And now she is in the bathroom with the old, wooden-handled kitchen knife and all is quiet, but for an occasional shallow moan and I tell her darling, please, please just pass me the knife. Please just tell me you are okay. I can't leave you here alone. And the neighbours, feeling a charitable responsibility towards Sonia, are intervening. Calling Anesh's parents, saying that though she is fatherless, Sonia is a sweet girl and a good match for their mentally ill son. She won't run away from him (a lie) and will make a good daughter.

They tell Sonia this. Two days later when the kitchen knife is returned to the kitchen and silver bangles chime across the scratches on her wrists. Then with dignity summoned from her very bone marrow she does not thank them, but states shortly and strongly, He is a *pagal wallah*, but I am not.

To be *pagal* is to be crazy. One who has lost their mind.

And now it is morning time again and without the red bucket, we scrub the bed sheets with hard brushes on the ground, a soapy line of water trailing across the concrete and down the steps. We peg them on the low metal threads that crown the rooftop and feel the warmth of the day gather its strength.

The matchmaking neighbour is herself getting married. She has burst out in all variety of new fashionable attire and developed a sudden wisdom regarding love. It is an arranged marriage. He is a non-resident Indian in Germany and she is burning through phone cards every night on the rooftop.

Swathed in pink chiffon and ankles clanking with bells, she offers Sonia some advice. Men want a wife, yar. Not girlfriends. They want a simple girl. Everyone is happier once they are married.

Later Sonia confides privately, what men want is oral sex. Sometimes anal, and they are happier when their bride has a good family and a motorbike as part of the dowry. Everything else is misery.

(On Dinesh's wedding night he phoned Sonia. Drunk. His slightly overweight and recently-deflowered bride lying awake at his side. She is fat, yar, and smelly between the legs. I miss you. I miss your sex.)

She missed his money and desperately, desperately missed his love.

Sometimes in my life, I feel I am a *pagal wallah*.

Above our little rooftop home, knotted power lines dissect the stars. Drying clothes folded over railings look set to jump.

# A. S. PATRIC

## *Cinders & bugs*

She was crying in line at the Post Office. Too close to me. Every
time we moved forward a step or two, I hoped she would take the
space to settle herself—or spread out her grief—but she pressed
forward. I wondered how far my charade of deafness would
stretch. Her tears came with words for her companion. A man
who told her to be quiet; that they'd talk about it later.

She was persistent in her grief, which trembled with an anger
that had, for the most part, been beaten out of her. Violence is
a heat and it wafted from her like a house almost burned to the
ground. Her words were cinders burning what was left standing.

We moved another few centimetres. And another step, together.
She pressed her sobs into the back of my head and said that the
man had been cruel talking about the bugs in her hair. The man
shooshed her. She washed regularly, she said, and telling people
she had bugs in her hair was a hurtful lie.

She was whimpering while I continued my deaf man pantomime,
perfected my performance as a bloke simply waiting in line, as
though I wasn't disgusted or afraid, but I could feel those bugs
hopping up and down below my ears.

---

# Minerva Blues

Minerva looks exactly like a fly these days. That's what happens when no one prays to you—diminishment and disgrace. Even so, (and it's certainly a credit to her former dignity and prestige) the goddess does not drone or buzz as she flies through my window. She whistles a tune called *Emily Dickinson Blues*, and I hum along for a few bars, before I swat her into a splotch of ink-black insect afterlife.

You can't kill divinities as easily as this, I know, but there is a brief moment in which I feel Olympian. I lean forward and peer into the entrails of the dead fly and the cosmos reveals its secrets. And yes, everything is very, very clear, but I have already forgotten the lovely tune Minerva was whistling only a few moments ago.

I have spent years trying to recall how it goes, and live with my windows wide open—even at the height of summer. Mosquitoes of Mesoamerican lineage leave a Braille of bites across my flesh but I cannot read Aztec or Inca. All I know is that they were once high priests who had surgical tastes for the human heart.

I gather with these late night whisperers of blood hunger, out by a streetlight that never sees any traffic. I suppose it has been put here for people like me, wandering around half-naked, on overly hot evenings. A moth flutters down from the yellow plastic illumination and tells me it used to visit the moon when its best friend was Mercury. Now we can't hear the stars and we can barely even see the constellations. I let the moth rest on my shoulder. Later, it tells me about the many ways civilisations reach their natural ends.

I shoo the moth away and know that I will soon forget. My memories are too many and so they turn themselves into fireflies. They drift away in a mass—resembling the cosmos swirling into the opposite of infinity. I should have found a jar and filled it with these lights. I might have kept a few recollections.

# VIVIENNE PLUMB

## *fish*

we bought the fish in the Rotorua Pak'n'Save to cook for dinner/
Mihi was serving behind the counter and she told us how she
teaches all day and then works in Pak'n'Save until ten at night
because her husband has no job/ she had spent that day in court
with two of her students/ fourteen years of age/ they had bashed
a man/ Mihi said it was not looking good for anyone/ it was pearl
fish that we bought/ it was Tuesday/ remember/ this is the day
the fresh fish comes in

# The alternative plan

Plan A: leave town. Plan B: stay in town but move to another part where no one knows you. Plan C: stay in the old apartment in the old part of town. Plan D: stay in the old apartment and in the old job. Plan E: look for a flatmate. Plan F: look for a new job. Plan G: change apartments within the same building. Plan H: stay in the old apartment in the same part of town, don't change your job and refuse to look for a flatmate. Plan I: go to Cuba (this plan requires an injection of money to activate it). Plan J: think of another plan. Plan K: get facial surgery (finance dependent). Plan L: dye your hair. Plan M: go out wearing a variety of hats. Plan N: stay indoors. Plan O: become a recluse. Plan P: become a recluse and stay in the same apartment and in the same part of town and in the same job. Plan Q: never say never. Plan R: this is something to do with running. Plan S: this must be swimming. Plan T: swimming every day and long walks in the weekend. Plan U: with your hair dyed. Plan V: and wearing a variety of hats. Plan W: become a recluse in the same apartment and in the same part of town but walk every Saturday in disguise and swim once a week (not in disguise). Plan X: change nothing. Plan Y: do not walk, run, or swim, but stay in the same manky apartment in the same scodey part of town, flogging yourself in the same boring job, and dream of Cuba. Plan Z: begin your plan for next year.

---

# The cinematic experience

In the movies men and women on bicycles in the spring always means sex. If he takes his hat off, he is either being polite, or he means to stay. If she takes her shoes off, it's either sex or a comedy. A cat will indicate a tedious storyline. Something is about to happen. Like a fish bone caught in its throat. The appearance of a kitten is the same. But worse. The removal of clothes will indicate either sex or a hospital scene. Or possibly sex in a hospital. Hospitals are a big clue that someone will die, unless it is a comedy. A walk in the park is never that straightforward. Children are used in the script to hear voices, see ghosts, become lost, scream, or to tap-dance. Babies ditto, but double all of the above.

## *the intercity*

i cannot believe i have slept through Levin/ our bus is like a needle
as it criss-crosses the pasture/ paddock/ fir/ forest/ foreshore of
New Zealand/ here comes the rain again the wet sheep stand
blinking in it/ one passenger wipes the steamed-up window with
her ugly turquoise window curtain/ i knew those bus curtains
were good for something

# ADEN ROLFE

## *The end of things*

The future is a fifteen-mile beach on the southern ocean, with rips and crosscurrents, waves crashing on each other from different directions. It's your footsteps being swallowed by a tide that's neither rising nor receding. It's trying to retrace your tracks to where they leave the waterline, up over the dune, figuring out which path to take through the scrub. There are signs of others' experience here—some footprints, not yours; dog tracks; faded cans and bottles—but all as if long abandoned.

I pick up some shells, because that's what you do at times like these, in places like these. I pick out ones that catch my eye: black-striped ones, large ones with flashes of purple and salmon, ones with orange sunbursts. Essentially, I choose the more distinct shells, but it's a flawed approach. The sand abounds in white and cream-coloured ones, shaped like small fans, yet I come away with atypical souvenirs, a non-representative sample.

Either way, I have no desire for shells. Later I'll put them in a box, give them away, discard them. But I'd do the same again, because that's how it works. I'd return to walk the shore, make footprints, pick out shells. We're drawn to these scenes—where everything is salted, bleached and breaking down —because they feel like the edge of something. Like the world is reaching up to reclaim things, that it could overwhelm you at any moment. And that's what you want, all there is left to feel.

Soon enough, the dusk turns each footstep into mound and shadow, indistinguishable from all the other indentations in the sand.

# MICHAEL SHARKEY

## *The strong, the silent type*

There was a woman who loved a man so much that she let herself go—bad?—o, shocking. He told her, 'Your feet push against me at night. Cut them off.' And she did, and she asked him if he slept well. He said, 'When you turn in the bed, your arms brush against me. Lose them.' And she did, and she lay there and asked him if he slept easier. He said, 'Sure, but often you talk far too much. Could you cut off your head?' So she organised that. And the man she loved slept like a top.

# A musical offering

Every time Scarlatti's songs and operas speak of poison he resorts to F-sharp minor. When the score speaks of delusion, you will hear A-major chords. Whenever Handel introduces monsters, say, Polyphemus the one-eyed into *Acis and Galatea*, you will hear stochastic notes. I'm looking for the perfect gift for visitors who ask me if I'm busy. Say a boxed set of baroque songs in A-major, F-sharp minor and a jumble of stray notes.

# LAURIE STEED

## *But what have you done lately?*

I knew this girl well not a girl more a woman named Amy and she made me want to love her right or wrong but to her love was a weakness sadness creeping in all over her skin into my mind and I said why don't we take a trip up the coast but it takes money to travel the coast so I sold my car and my furniture and my cds and thought yes love is blind but she's behind me as we board the plane and we're going to build a brand new life just me and my future wife.

We got to Queensland in its coldest winter how cold well the koalas had frostbite and we were looking after two dogs Bonnie and Rex well I say we but I was home and Amy was in nightclubs slamming shot after shot with her sister who wasn't her sister but they called each other sister cause Amy's real sister lived in a flat where the door was blocked up with mail paper anything really so long as the front door stayed firmly shut and she believed in many things but she didn't like to party like you can't party no more and when you can't party no more you fall down so I looked after the dogs while she crawled on the bar floor trying to find a lost earring and be careful on that floor you don't know where it's been and then she's back in bed with the hiccoughs and she runs to the bathroom leaving dashes of pink along the hallway carpet.

We could never drive too far or our car would overheat so we carried fifteen-litre bottles of water and poured them in the radiator and come on car we're barely out of Brisbane but it's had enough and it only cools down when the heater is on and we only have one cd it's *eyes open* by Snow Patrol and if you listen to this album and you listen to the songs you think you are listening to the same song over and over but that's the joke this album is the same feeling over and over and if I lay here if I just lay here Amy might tell me she's glad I made the trip that she appreciates me selling all my things to be with her and she likes the time we're spending but she's not glad no not at all but I am all she has so naturally she wants to tear me apart.

Amy has long black hair and piercing green eyes and when you take a photo her face changes and she says she loves *alias* and that's a good show for someone who is constantly pretending to be someone else and when she's drunk she tries to fight me but I'm not fighting hard enough she wants me to attack her like in a movie but this is not a movie its my life and all I want is for Amy to be okay but it's like wanting glasses not to break or Snow Patrol to sound less like Coldplay and more like the Yeah Yeah Yeahs but Amy loves me I know she loves me I have it written down so if she loves me then why am I writing this story?

I knew this girl well more a woman named Amy and we drove up the coast only we weren't together at that point just strangers in a car listening to the same song but if I lay here if I just lay here can you take me back to Perth and I was young but not so young that I should have been flying across the country chasing a woman who was never there just a ghost or once she was amazing but she drifted out and you could never work out why she was angry she was just really angry and I took a photo of her with a big mango and she said they're shooting *Australia* here and I nodded though she meant in Bowen and I meant in our car and the water is bubbling and the songs sound the same but when its time we will overflow and we'll leave the car and when we reach Cairns I will get on the bus and just before I go we'll be together for the first time in our relationship it's not just a moment but the exact moment because you only see the moment when it's about to end.

Amy says she loves me.

And I believe her.

# SEAN WILSON

## *Silver fox*

She was asleep in the passenger seat of his car. The sun was low ahead as he turned the steering wheel left and right along the snaking Great Ocean Road. Below reinforced steel barriers, waves rolled slowly toward the brown and grey-streaked rocks. Clouds the colour of hotel sheets moved in from the west. He had his window all the way down. He liked the breeze rushing by. The feeling brought back memories of his childhood—pedalling his bike down steep bitumen hills, racing his friends, screaming with abandon. He was amused but felt lonesome. It was a memory for a boy who no longer existed, a feeling no longer available. It was a reminder of the many ordinary absences time had created in his life. The road turned to cut between two hills and the ocean disappeared.

She was to leave in three days for Philadelphia to start a new job. He was not going with her.

The car hit a pothole and the jolt woke her. She breathed deeply and licked her lips. 'How long was I out?'

He shook his head and raised his eyebrows. 'Pretty much since the engine started,' he said, 'as always.'

The road sent them south again and ocean filled the windows. She rubbed the skin around her eyes hard as if peeling paint. He heard her breathe in the ocean air like steam from a meal.

'I had the weirdest dream,' she said. 'Better than the one where that cat jumped in front of a bullet to save my life.'

'Let's hear it,' he said.

'Well, it was all about you,' she said. 'One day, your hair went completely white like you were an eighty-year-old man and suddenly you became Prime Minister.' She laughed suddenly, quickly as she remembered. 'You didn't earn it,' she said, 'You didn't work hard. Your hair went white and then you became the youngest ever Prime Minister. A bit like Doogie Howser but instead of studying hard, you got the job because of your hair colour.'

He rubbed his temples like he was kneading bread. The previous night's office Christmas party drinks had passed quickly through his body, scraping his head and chest, leaving everything raw. When he had crept with heavy feet into the bedroom he found her asleep. As he pulled back the sheets, he had reached out to wake her but had changed his mind.

'When do you think you'll go grey?'

'I already am going grey,' he said.

'No, not this salt and pepper thing,' she said, reaching out and flicking his hair. 'When do you think you'll go proper grey?'

'I don't know,' he said. He ran his fingers through his hair.

'When did you get your first grey hairs?'

'Nineteen,' he said.

'Nineteen!' she said. 'Most people are still growing and you'd already started to decline. Were you scared?'

'No, I was excited,' he said. 'All my friends were older and I wanted to be like them—grey hairs, beards and all.'

The road turned toward a thick wood of trees that had grown with the wind, leaning away from the sea, trunks stuck in a stumble. 'When do you think I'll go grey?' he said.

She smiled, turning to face him. 'Are we making a bet?' she said.

'Sure, why not?'

She squinted and tapped her bottom lip. 'Forty-five,' she said, 'give or take.'

'I say forty,' he said.

'That's not so far away,' she said. 'You've got a lot of aging to do.'

'You'll have to stick around,' he said, 'and see who wins.'

She began to laugh but stopped suddenly. She moved her hair away from her eyes, behind her ear, and turned from him. She looked out the window, her eyes tracing the paths of squat shrubs and leaning trees.

'Okay,' she said. 'Can we be friends until then?'

'You mean you'll only come back to me when I'm completely grey?' he said.

She smiled and turned toward him, blinking quickly. 'A silver fox, yeah,' she said. 'I'll write you emails until you're 45 to find out how it's coming along.'

'You'll need to keep in touch,' he said. 'My guess was 40, remember?'

---

'I remember,' she said. She rubbed her hand on the bare skin below her dress. 'The sooner the better,' she said.

They reached a small town—a few weathered shops beside a beach. He turned the car toward the tourist information stand and parked. She got out quickly, stretching her legs and groaning. An older couple stood in front of the stand. He watched them for a moment, the hair on each whiter than the sand. They stood side by side reading the stand, their elbows touching.

'Who do you think won that bet?' he said but she didn't hear.

# ACKNOWLEDGEMENTS

Allison, Dael. 'Nightburst' is published in *Adrift*, a chapbook of Northern Territory poets, 2010, and on A Writer a Day, Varuna, The Writers' House 2011.

Beveridge, Judy. 'The book of birds' and 'Address from the Curved City' from *The Domesticity of Giraffes*, Black Lightning Press, 1987.

Boyle, Peter. 'In response to a critic's call for tighter editing'. from *Museum of Space*, UQP, 2004.

burns, joanne. 'literate' first published in *Perihelion Review USA*, Winter 2010.

Cahill, Michelle. 'An exercise in magic realism' first appeared on her blog, Negative Capability.

Hammial, Philip. 'Gold', 'Milk', 'Tony's museum' and 'Traps' from *Swan Song*, Picaro Press, 2004.

Plumb, Vivienne. 'fish' from *crumple*, Seraph Press, NZ, 2010. 'The alternative plan' and 'The cinematic experience' from *Nefarious*, HeadworX, NZ, 2004. 'the intercity' from *The Cheese and Onion Sandwich and Other New Zealand Icons*, Seraph Press, NZ, 2012.

Sharkey, Michael. 'The strong, the silent type' from *The Sweeping Plain*, Five Islands Press, 2007.

# BIOGRAPHIES

**Dael Allison** writes poems, essays and memoir. *Fairweather Raft*, her poems exploring the life of wandering artist Ian Fairweather, will be published by Walleah Press in 2012. Like Fairweather she is inclined to drift away.

**Judith Beveridge** has published four books of poetry. Her most recent collection is *Storm and Honey*, Giramondo, 2009. She is the poetry editor for *Meanjin* and teaches poetry at post graduate level at The University of Sydney.

**Peter Boyle** lives in Sydney. His *New and Selected Poetry* is due out with Puncher and Wattmann in 2012.

**joanne burns**'s most recent book is *amphora*, Giramondo Publishing, 2011. Her work was represented in the *Indigo Book of Australian Prose Poems*, Ginninderra Press, 2011. She has been writing in the prose poem form for many years.

**Michelle Cahill's** stories have appeared in *Southerly*, *TEXT* and *Etchings*, forthcoming in *Antipodes*. She received a Literature Board grant to write fiction at Sanskriti Kendra. Her recent publications are *Vishvarüpa*, Five Islands Press and *Night Birds*, Vagabond.

**John Carey** is an ex-teacher of French and Latin and a former actor. He is the author of three poetry collections, the latest *The Old Humanists*, Puncher & Wattmann, 2009.

**Julie Chevalier** has written *Permission to Lie*, Spineless Wonders, 2011 and *linen tough as history*, Puncher & Wattmann, 2012. *Darger: his girls*, winner of the Alec Bolton Prize 2012, is forthcoming. http://juliechevalier.net

---

**Shady Cosgrove** is a senior lecturer in Creative Writing at the University of Wollongong. Her fiction has appeared in *Overland*, *Southerly*, *Antipodes* and *Best Australian Stories*. She is the author of the book *She Played Elvis*, Allen and Unwin, 2009.

**Moya Costello** has published two collections of short creative prose and one novella. She teaches Writing in the School of Arts and Social Sciences, Southern Cross University.

**Anna Couani** is a Sydney writer and secondary ESL teacher. Her most recent book, *Small Wonders*, 2012 is poetry with Chinese translations and drawings. Her published work is at: http:// seacruise.ath.cx/annacouani

**Charles D'Anastasi** is a Melbourne poet. He has had poems published in various journals. He has a particular interest in the prose poem. His chapbook *The unreliable harbour* was published by the Melbourne Poets Union.

**Michael Farrell** coedited (with Jill Jones) *Out of the Box: Contemporary Australian Gay and Lesbian Poets*. His latest publication is *thou sand* from Tinfish.

**Adam Ford's** novel, three poetry collections and short story collection can be sampled at www.theotheradamford.wordpress. com. He lives in Chewton.

**Keri Glastonbury** is a lecturer in Creative Writing at The University of Newcastle. Her poetry collection *grit salute* will be published in 2012 by SOI3.

**Linda Godfrey** is an editor and publicist for Spineless Wonders, hosts the poetry event Rocket Readings, can't resist a prose poem, has a Masters of Professional Writing from the University of Technology, Sydney.

**Monica Goldberg** is a surrealist writer and artist. She has taught writing in community centres and has worked as a photographer. Her first novel is about the significance of cryptic faith.

**Erin Gough**'s short stories have been published in a number of journals and collections, including *Southerly*, *Overland*, *Going Down Swinging* and *Best Australian Stories*, and have been read on ABC and 2ser radio.

**Gregory A Gould** studied Creative Writing at the University of Canberra and is the co-founder of Blemish Books. He grew up in far north Queensland.

**Philip Hammial** has had twenty-four collections of poetry published, two of which were short-listed for the Kenneth Slessor Prize and one for the ACT Poetry Prize.

**Stu Hatton** is a Melbourne-based poet and editor who teaches writing and editing at Deakin University. His debut collection, *How to Be Hungry*, is available through http://www.stuhatton. net.

**Paden Hunter** is one of Sydney's young creatives. As well as his illustration work for Spineless Wonders he has turned his talents to theatre design and is an exhibited artist. He is completing a Bachelor of Design at COFA.

**Carol Jenkins**'s first book *Fishing in the Devonian*, Puncher & Wattmann, 2008, was shortlisted for the Victorian Premier's and Anne Elder Awards. Next is *Exit Speed*, due out from Puncher & Wattmann in 2012.

**Jo Langdon** is a literary studies PhD candidate at Deakin University. She writes short fiction and poetry, and a chapbook of her poems, *Snowline*, will be published in early 2012 by Whitmore Press.

**Kent MacCarter** is Managing Editor of Cordite Poetry Review, an executive board member of SPUNC, an active member in Melbourne PEN and lives in Victoria with his wife, son and two cats.

**Clare McHugh** is a Canberra-based writer and editor. She has published pieces in *First*, 2006 and 2009 and 'Unexpected' in *The Sound of Silence*, 2011.

**Bronwyn Mehan** lives in Sydney. Her fiction and poetry have appeared in *The Age, Island, Meanjin* and *Southerly*. She is founder of Spineless Wonders.

**Alyson Miller** lives in Geelong and has recently completed a PhD in scandalous literature at Deakin University. Her short stories and poetry have appeared in *Staples, Verandah* and *Eureka Street*.

**Cara Munro** is a registered nurse. Her work has appeared in *Eureka Street* and the book, *Learnings–Lessons we are learning about living together*. She won the 2009 Margaret Dooley Award.

**Alec Patric** is the author of *The Rattler & other stories*, Spineless Wonders, 2011. He is published in *Best Australian Stories* and in 2011, he won the Ned Kelly, SD Harvey Short Story Award and the Booranga Short Story Prize.

**Vivienne Plumb** writes poetry, drama, and fiction. Her collections include *Nefarious: poems and parables*, 2004, *crumple*, 2010 and *The Cheese and Onion Sandwich and Other New Zealand Icons*, 2011.

**Aden Rolfe** is a writer, editor and radiomaker. His poetry has appeared in *Overland* and *Best Australian Poems 2009* and *2010*. His radio works have been broadcast on ABC Radio National.

**Michael Sharkey** is a poet and biographer who lives in Armidale, NSW. He taught literature in universities in Australia and abroad and has reviewed books for newspapers and journals in Australia and New Zealand.

**Laurie Steed** is a New Zealand-born, Australian-raised writer, editor and reviewer. He has appeared in various literary journals and is currently completing his PhD in Creative Writing at the University of Western Australia.

**Sean Wilson**'s writing has appeared in *Wet Ink* and *Cottonmouth: An Anthology of New Australian Writing*. He was one of the editors of *stop drop and roll*. He lives in Melbourne.

---

Other books from Spineless Wonders

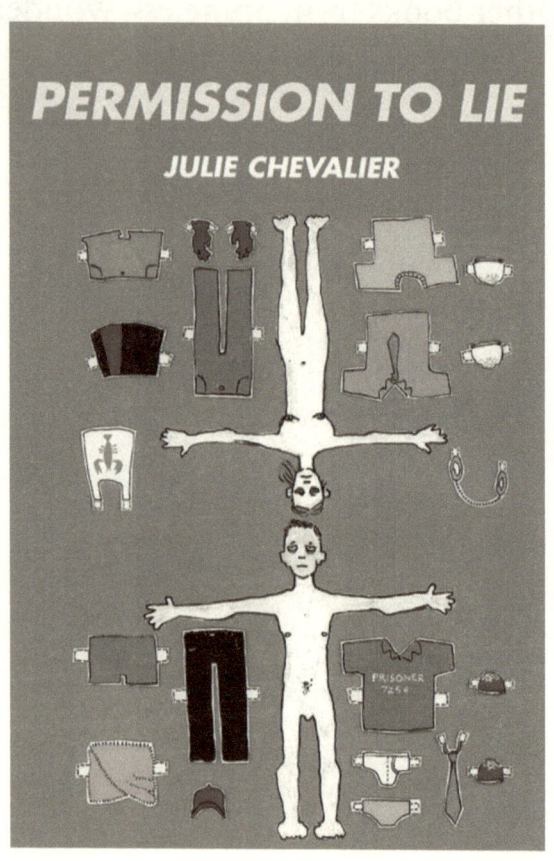

# PERMISSION TO LIE

### JULIE CHEVALIER

# Permission to Lie
## by Julie Chevalier

In this wonderfully diverse collection, Chevalier does not flinch from delving into some of the messier aspects of contemporary Australian culture, whether inside prisons, nudist camps or in cut-throat boardrooms.

Cover art and six pages of quirky illustrations by Paden Hunter.

> 'Holding together the extensive range of this collection is prose of a deceptive simplicity, taut, droll, hinting at greater depths, never giving too much away. A new voice in Australian fiction, wry, gritty, knowing and true.'

**Fiona McGregor**
author of **Indelible Ink**

# The Rattler
### & other stories

## A.S. Patrić

"Spare and taut, sometimes tricky, sometimes shocking, yet always
deeply and satisfyingly tender. A great collection."
Paddy O'Reilly

# The Rattler
# & other stories
## by A.S. Patrić

This entertaining collection includes a romp of a novella called *The Rattler*, as well as short stories and microfiction all set in and around contemporary Melbourne. Sometimes serious, sometimes seriously playful— always written in breathtakingly beautiful prose—these stories uncover the heartbreaking tragedies, slow-burning emotions and the serendipity of ordinary lives. Cover art and illustrations by Miles Allinson. Collage by Maxine Beneba Clarke.

*'An explosive mix of muscular prose and sharp originality. In this collection, A.S. Patric proves himself to be a writer who must be taken very seriously.'*

**Vanessa Gebbie**
UK author of ***Short Circuit, A Guide to the Art of the Short Story***

Quality short fiction, packed with surprises.
Prepare to be transported.   Marion Halligan

# ESCAPE

*An anthology of
short stories*

# Escape An anthology of short stories

## edited by Bronwyn Mehan

Here is the thinking person's escapist reading. ESCAPE has unexpected tales of contemporary life, comedy, tragedy, mystery, romance, sci-fi, dystopian fantasy, a homage to David Foster Wallace and lots more. All served with a good dose of quirky and a fine turn of phrase. Features award-winning writers such as Ryan O'Neill, Jen Mills, Andy Kissane, Louise Swinn, Julie Chevalier, A.S. Patrić and Kim Westwood, as well as stories chosen by Sophie Cunningham in the inaugural Carmel Bird Short Fiction Award.

Contains illustrations by talented young artist, Paden Hunter.

> *'Quality fiction.'*
> **Kerryn Goldsworthy**
> critic, **Sydney Morning Herald**

"A startling collection... sly humour and memorable characters."
-CHRIS WOMERSLEY

# PIERZ NEWTON-JOHN
# FAULT LINES

Returns the grit to the
Australian literary landscape
-MATTHEW CONDON

# Fault Lines

## byPierz Newton-John

Seamless prose, undercurrents of contemporary music, the urbane writing, the suburban settings, but it is all happening behind closed doors.

> 'Newton-John's astonishing collection of stories is both a thing of beauty and the stuff of nightmares. Here is a visceral contemporary world populated with predators, uncertain hearts, the damned and the hopeful, grasping for love and meaning at the edge of what we might call ordinary existence.
>
> Here are the fault lines in all our lives, and Newton-John, with an unflinching eye and a mesmerising style, lays them bare in this sequence of expertly crafted vignettes. Fault Lines returns the grit to the Australian literary landscape.'

**Matthew Condon**
author of **Trout Opera**